DEC 0 1 1998	DATE DUE		
T6			
TA			
T40			
T 16			

To Erin
Christmas 1989
From "Gu Gu & Pata"

Martha's Best Friend

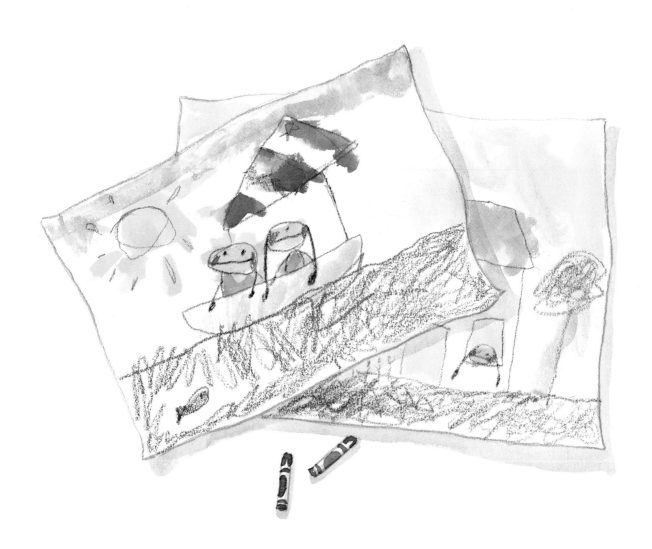

Danielle Steel
Martha's
Best Friend

Illustrated by Jacqueline Rogers

Delacorte Press

Published by
Delacorte Press
Bantam Doubleday Dell Publishing Group, Inc.
666 Fifth Avenue
New York, New York 10103

Library of Congress Cataloging in Publication Data

Steel, Danielle.
   Martha's best friend / by Danielle Steel; illustrated by Jacqueline Rogers.
     p. cm.
   Summary: A new girl from Paris arrives to spend the year at Martha's school and they become very good friends.
   ISBN 0-385-29801-3
   [1. Schools—Fiction. 2. Friendship—Fiction.] I. Rogers, Jacqueline, ill. II. Title.
PZ7.S8143Mak 1989
[E]—dc19   88-35250
                                      CIP
                                       AC

design by Judith Neuman-Cantor

Manufactured in the United States of America

November 1989

10 9 8 7 6 5 4 3 2 1

To Sammie, my very, very special little girl, with the big, big heart, who hates to say good-bye, just as much as I do. This story is for you, with all my love,
Mommy.

And to some very special friends: Inee; Rome; Lucy; Nanny Phillips; Jean; Nicola; Madeleine; Camilla; and Lynda. With love, and special thanks to all of you. Never say good-bye . . . only au revoir *. . . You will be in our hearts forever.*

With love,
d.s.

This is Martha. She lives in San Francisco, where there is a very crooked street, lots of hills, cable cars, a beautiful bay, and the Golden Gate Bridge.

Martha has blue eyes and curly blond hair, and some freckles. She lives in a very old house on Russian Hill. There is an old firehouse right on her block, and an old schoolhouse, and an octagonal house (that means it's a house that has eight sides).

Martha likes wearing pretty dresses and party shoes best of all, and her very favorite shoes are red.

Martha wishes she could wear her
red shoes to school. But she knows that
she has to wear her school uniform. She
is five years old, and she's in kindergarten.
   Martha has lots of friends in school
and her favorite day is Show and Tell.
   One day, just before Show and Tell,
something interesting happened at

Martha's school. A new girl arrived. She
had straight brown hair that she wore
in two long braids tied with pink ribbons,
big brown eyes, and she wasn't smiling.
She looked very serious, and a little
scared. Martha noticed right away that
she was wearing shiny black patent
leather shoes that Martha thought were
very pretty.

"Good morning, everyone," Mrs. Higgins said. She was the head of the school. "This is Madeleine. She's come all the way from Paris." Everyone stared at her and no one was sure where Paris was, except that it sounded far away, from the way Mrs. Higgins said it. "Paris is in France. Madeleine has come to live here for the school year. And next summer she's going back home, but by then, we'll all be good friends, won't we?"

Martha watched Madeleine as she sat down at a desk in a corner of the classroom. A little while later, she saw Madeleine watching her. She looked frightened, but Martha thought she was pretty.

At recess, when it was time for milk
and cookies, Martha walked over to
Madeleine. "Hi," she said. Madeleine
looked down at her shiny black shoes
and whispered, *"Bonjour,"* which is
"Hello" in French.

"Do you speak English?" Martha asked,
finishing her last cookie.

Madeleine looked up with her big brown
eyes and smiled. *"Un peu* . . . a little
bit." She had a little accent, and Martha
decided right away that she liked it.

"Would you like to see the playhouse?"
Madeleine nodded. Martha took her over
to the dolls. There were dress-up clothes,
too, given by some of the Mommies, and
doll carriages, lots of pretend food,
shopping carts, and a blue telephone,
which Martha liked to play with.

Martha and Madeleine played there
for a long time. Later, they went out into
the playground. Martha showed Madeleine
the swings and the seesaw. And they
went down the slide one after the other.
When Madeleine's Mommy came to pick
her up, Martha waved at them as she
drove away in her car pool.

The next day, they were excited to see each other again. They played on the swings and the seesaw. And when there weren't enough cookies for everyone, because someone had made a mistake that day, Martha shared half her cookie with Madeleine. And by the end of the week, they were best friends.

Martha had her Mommy call Madeleine's
Mommy so they could play after school
at each other's houses.

That weekend, they took a ride on the
cable car, and went to Fisherman's Wharf
and Ghirardelli Square, and Madeleine
told Martha all about Paris.

She told her about the Eiffel Tower, and the Arc de Triomphe, and the Luxembourg Gardens, where she used to play. She also told about the Bois de Boulogne, where they used to walk their dog. He was too big, so they had had to leave him in Paris. Next summer they were going home, but that was a long, long time away.

Madeleine confessed that she missed her *Grandmaman,* that was her grandmother in French, and her house, and her bed, and her own room, and her dog.

She had come to San Francisco with her parents because her Daddy had to do some work there, and her brother, Pierre, had come too, but Madeleine said he was really awful. Once he told her that a monster was going to eat her up, and once he hid under her bed, and then jumped up and scared Madeleine while she was dressing her doll. Their Mommy had scolded him, and Martha was glad she didn't have a brother.

Pierre spoke English well. He played soccer on weekends. When he grew up, he said, he was going to fly an airplane. Madeleine was going to be a nurse. Martha said she just wanted to be a Mommy.

The time passed. Martha took Madeleine trick-or-treating for the first time, because they don't have Halloween in Paris.

And at Thanksgiving, Madeleine and her Mommy and Daddy and Pierre came to Martha's house for turkey dinner. Martha lived there with her Mommy. Her Mommy and Daddy had gotten divorced two years before, which meant they weren't married anymore. But Martha's Daddy lived in a house nearby, and she saw him very often, like on Wednesday nights and on weekends. And Martha spent the weekend with her Daddy after Thanksgiving, and he took her and Madeleine to the movies.

At Christmas, Martha and her Mommy went to Madeleine's house, and Madeleine's Mommy played the piano and sang French Christmas carols. Some of the songs were the same, except for the words, which were in French.

At Easter, Martha and Madeleine
were both bunnies in the school play.
They hopped all over the stage together.
They had fun coloring Easter eggs, eating
jelly beans, and making Easter baskets
for their friends.

Soon it was time for school to end.
There was a party at school for Madeleine
on the last day, because in September,
when all the other children came back to
school after the summer, Madeleine
would be back in Paris. "It's a good-bye
party," Annie, one of their friends,
explained. "How do you say good-bye in
French?"

    "You say it two ways in French,"
Madeleine told the other children at
her party. "You can say *adieu,* which
means good-bye forever, or *au revoir,*
which means until we meet again. Most
of the time, we say *au revoir.*" The
teacher wrote it on the blackboard.
Everyone looked at the words.

All the children gave Madeleine cards they had made with their pictures on them, so that she would always remember them. They put a picture of Madeleine up on the corkboard, so they would remember her.

"I will miss you when I'm back in Paris," she said sadly.

"Will you write to us?" the children asked.

"Yes, will you write to me?"

"Of course!" Everyone promised to write letters.

On the way home to Russian Hill that afternoon, Martha was very quiet. She was alone in the car with her Mommy. Martha told her about Madeleine's party. Her Mommy knew she was sad about Madeleine going back to France. But she wasn't leaving for a while yet. Not until after the Fourth of July.

The time went quickly now, too quickly for Martha. On the Fourth of July, there was a big picnic.

Martha and her Mommy and Madeleine and Pierre and their parents, and all their friends went to it. There were lots of children and parents, lots of fried chicken and corn on the cob, and hamburgers and hot dogs and apple pie and pickles. Some people sang and some people played the guitar. Everyone had a good time.

At night fireworks lit up the sky. It was the most beautiful thing Martha and Madeleine had ever seen, even if Pierre did say a dragon was going to fall out of the sky and eat them.

As they watched the beautiful fireworks, Madeleine and Martha held hands because they were very best friends.

On the way home in the car, they fell asleep, still holding hands, with their heads on each other's shoulders.

But the next morning, when Martha came down to breakfast, she was very quiet. Her Mommy thought she was still tired from the night before, but she wasn't. She was thinking. It was July fifth, and the next day Madeleine and Pierre and their parents were leaving. Martha felt as if there were a rock in her heart.

That afternoon Madeleine and her Mommy came for a last visit.
The Mommies drank tea in the kitchen. Martha and Madeleine played, but it wasn't the same. All Martha could think about was how terrible it was that Madeleine was leaving.

But when their Mommies came out of the kitchen, Martha's Mommy was smiling. "Do you know what we've decided?" she asked. "I think we're going to Paris to visit Madeleine next summer!" The girls jumped up and down and clapped. But when they said good-bye that afternoon, next summer seemed like a long time away.

All Martha could think about was that Madeleine was leaving. Martha felt as if her heart would break when she kissed Madeleine good-bye. Who would she play with now? Who would ride home with her in her car pool? And what if Madeleine never came back, or forgot to write, or couldn't remember their address . . . what if they never saw her again? . . . or worse yet, what if she forgot them? It was the worst thing that had ever happened to Martha, she felt as though she were losing her very best friend, and she didn't want it to happen. But she knew that she couldn't stop her from leaving.

Madeleine's Mommy promised that they would write, and that they would come back again. And Martha's Mommy promised again that they would go to Paris.

Madeleine and Martha hugged and
kissed for a long time, and just before
Madeleine left, Martha ran upstairs and
brought back Patsy, one of her favorite
dolls. Patsy had on a blue dress and
a pink hat. Martha knew how much
Madeleine loved her. She gave her to
Madeleine. Madeleine held her tight as
she gave Martha another big hug and kiss.

She waved sadly as she got in the car
to go back to her house. The next
morning, Madeleine and her family
would be flying back to Paris.

"Don't forget us," Martha said, two big
tears rolling down her face, as she
waved good-bye.

"I'll always love you!" Madeleine was
crying too. Then she called, *"Au revoir."*
Martha and her Mommy waved until the
car turned the corner.

"I'll always love you too," Martha
whispered. Then she remembered the
words. *Au revoir,* until we meet again.
She could hardly wait until they went
to Paris.

Martha was sad for a long time. It was
an awful feeling to see her best friend
go away, and so far away too. But
Martha's Mommy promised that the next
summer they would go to Paris.

It was a long year, waiting to
see Madeleine again, but Martha and
Madeleine wrote each other lots of
letters, and their Mommies sent lots of
pictures. Finally, when school was over
the following year, Martha and her
Mommy got on a plane and went to
Paris.

Madeleine and her Mommy and Daddy
and Pierre were at the airport waiting
for them. Martha was so excited, she
could hardly stand it. Both girls had
grown a lot, and so had Pierre. He
seemed a lot nicer. He was waving a
little American flag at the airport. The
girls jumped into each other's arms.

Madeleine's Daddy drove them around
Paris on the way home and showed them
everything. They all talked and laughed
and tried to tell everything that had
happened in a whole year. In the
backseat, Madeleine and Martha held
hands while Pierre waved a little
American flag out the window.

Martha and her Mommy stayed in
Paris for two weeks and Martha bought
lots of postcards to show her Daddy
when she went back to San Francisco.

They had a wonderful time. When it
was time to leave, Martha and Madeleine
were sad, but they knew that they'd be
together again soon. And best of all, they
knew they'd always be friends. And they
were, right until they were grown-ups.